CW01186695

Alien Arrival

1971

Alien Arrival 1971

by W J Dewhurst

First published 2023.

Contact the author at alienarrival1971@gmail.com

ISBN: 9798865212775

Contents

Chapter One: Setting Off

‘Only ten minutes till take off!’ said Captain Smith.

‘We’d better get aboard,’ replied Professor Kowalski. 'Oh, yeah, I have just been reading the newspaper and it says there have been UFO sightings.'

‘There are no such things as aliens!’ Smith laughed.

Smith and Kowalski were going to explore the moon. Smith was an astronaut and fighter pilot. Kowalski was a scientist. It was a warm summer's day. Their rocket was waiting outside at an air base in California. They got in and ran the checks. When everything was ready, Captain Smith took off.

Three days later…

Professor Kowalski spoke into the radio. 'I'm going to explore behind those rocks.'

'Be careful!' replied Smith, who was still on board the rocket.

'What's this?'

'What's what?'

But Kowalski's radio had died. Smith decided he had to go and investigate. So he climbed out of the rocket and walked on the moon's surface. He followed Kowalski's footprints. Suddenly the footprints stopped behind the rocks. Kowalski had disappeared!

Smith looked all around the rocks, but Kowalski was gone. He kept looking, but found nothing. He went back to the rocket and got a shovel. Then he went back to the rocks and started digging. Eventually, he found a perfect circle carved into the moon rock.

'Hello, can you hear me, Sally? It's Captain Smith here.'

'Is everything OK?'

'Not really.'

'Why not?'

'Kowalski has disappeared. And under the dust, I've found a circle carved in the rock.'

‘That’s impossible. Who could have carved a circle?’

‘Did you send anyone else to the moon at the same time as us?’

‘No. You are the only ones on the moon that we know of.’

‘How strange? I think I’d better start digging.’

Smith got a pick axe from the rocket and started to dig away again around the circle. After a few minutes he had to take a break. While he was resting, he found a small lever. He decided to pull the lever and see what would happen. As soon as he pulled it, the circle moved into the moon rock leaving a hole in the ground.

Smith looked into the hole. He could see metal on the sides of a chute stretching down. If Smith was ever going to find

Kowalski, he had to go down the chute. So he jumped down and landed in an underground room. There was a faint light in the middle of the room, so Smith was able to look round. He saw a computer and some shelves with test tubes and other scientific equipment. It was obviously a lab. But still no Kowalski. In the corner there was another chute leading further down. So Smith decided to jump down.

Because of the moon's low gravity, Smith again easily landed in the next room. This room was very bright because of four long strip lights on the ceiling. At the other side of the room, there was a huge black eye that seemed to be scanning him and a computer. Smith tried to avoid the huge black eye as he went over to the computer. On the screen, he read:

SPECIES: HUMAN.

GENDER: MALE.

HAIR: BLOND.

EYES: BROWN.

HEIGHT: SIX FOOT ONE INCH.

CATEGORY: INTRUDER.

The last word, “Intruder”, was flashing.

‘Someone must know I’m here,’ thought Smith. ‘I need to find Kowalski quickly!’

Smith decided to jump down to the next room. The third room was also lit with strip lights and there were four purple containers shaped like bath tubs. They were filled with very hot purple liquid. Smith decided to go and look inside one of the bath tubs. When he got near, a green hand appeared out of the purple liquid.

'That's not a human!' thought Smith. 'Sally said there wasn't supposed to be anyone here.'

Chapter Two: Aliens?

'If there really are aliens here, Kowalski could be in danger,' thought Smith. There was only one way to go, down another chute to the fourth room. Smith ran to the chute and jumped down.

The next room looked like an engine room. Smith walked to a computer. On the screen it said:

CELL ONE: EMPTY.

CELL TWO: EMPTY.

CELL THREE: HUMAN, 1.

CELL FOUR: EMPTY.

CELL FIVE: EMPTY.

'That must be Kowalski in cell three,' thought Smith. 'Is he in a prison somewhere?' He noticed that all the cell doors could only be opened by aliens. Smith reprogrammed the cell doors so that humans and aliens could open them. He also found a bottle lying under the computer desk. It contained a glowing purple liquid. He decided to pick it up.

Then Smith jumped down the next chute. 'This must be the prison!' thought Smith. The room wasn't very bright because there was only one light. Smith saw Kowalski in one of the prison cells.

Kowalski signalled to Smith not to make a sound. Smith noticed two green figures talking to each other. They had big bold blackhole-like eyes and spoke in strange-sounding high-pitched voices. Luckily, they hadn't noticed him. Another green figure was on a computer.

Smith flicked the light switch off. It went dark. Smith heard quiet muttering from the green figures. In the darkness, Smith navigated to Kowalski's cell and opened the door.

'Thank goodness you found me,' whispered Kowalski. 'There's an elevator on the bottom floor.'

'We have to be quick, before the lights come back on!' whispered Smith.

Smith and Kowalski jumped down the chute and found an elevator. They hurried into the elevator and it took them to the surface. Smith and Kowalski ran back to the rocket and climbed in. Smith started the rocket and they took off.

'Hello, this is Smith.'

'Yes,' said Sally.

'I've found an underground alien base, I think.'

'Aliens?'

'Yes, aliens. They captured Kowalski, but I was able to rescue him. They put him in some sort of prison.'

'Kowalski was kidnapped by aliens and put in a prison?'

'Yes. That's all.'

'Can I speak to Kowalski?'

'Yes, you can.'

'Hello?' said Kowalski.

'Hello, Professor Kowalski,' said Sally. 'Captain Smith said that you were captured by aliens and put in a prison. Are you OK?'

'Yes, I'm fine.'

'Do you have any information about the aliens?'

'They don't speak English. They wanted to learn about our technology. That's why they kidnapped me, because I'm a scientist.'

'I wonder why they want to know about our technology.'

'I think they might try and invade the Earth.'

'Why do you think that?'

'I saw something on one of the computer screens about them trying to spy on us. It looks like there are already alien spies on Earth.'

Three days later…

‘Kowalski?’ said Smith. ‘We’re back.’

‘We need to think of a plan to stop the aliens from invading.’

‘What type of plan?’ asked Smith.

‘Tracking down the alien spies.’

‘How are we supposed to do that?’

‘We could make a detector.’

‘What type of detector?’

‘That detects the spies. The aliens bathe in radioactive liquid. If we detect radioactivity that might lead us to the aliens on Earth.’

Chapter Three: The Detector

Smith and Kowalski were in Kowalski's lab.

'What is that?' asked Smith.

'It's a detector,' said Kowalski.

'Is this for the alien spies?'

'Yes.' In his left hand Kowalski was holding a miniature satellite dish. In the other hand, he had a small tablet device. 'When aliens are 105 feet away, they will appear on this screen.'

‘How are we going to get close enough to detect them?’

‘We need to find where UFOs have been sighted.’

‘I’ll go and buy a few newspapers.’

‘I’ll wait for you here.’

Two hours later…

‘Look!’ said Smith, pointing at a page in one of the newspapers. ‘Here’s a report saying that flying saucers have been seen in Athens.’

‘Why would aliens have gone to Greece?’ wondered Kowalski.

‘Let’s find out!’ said Smith.

'We'd better get packing!' said Kowalski.

Two days later…

'We're here!' said Kowalski.

'Where in Athens are the aliens?' asked Smith.

'I arranged a meeting with the journalist who wrote about the UFOs. He may be able to tell us some more about the UFO sightings.'

Soon they were in the journalist's office.

'My name hello is Xenos,' said the journalist.

'Can you just wait a minute, I need to talk to my friend,' said Smith.

'OK.'

Smith and Kowalski stepped outside of the journalist's office.

'Kowalski,' said Smith. 'Xenos is Greek for alien.'

'Why would he be called alien?'

'Either he really loves writing about aliens… or he is one.'

Kowalski took the detector out of his lab coat and turned it on. The black screen showed some orange dots. 'That's you and me,' said Kowalski. 'The other orange dots are other people like us. But if we see a green dot that means there's an alien.'

A few seconds later a green dot appeared.

'Isn't that a green dot?' asked Smith.

'Yes. And it seems to be in the journalist's office. He must be an alien in disguise.'

'This must be a trap. The aliens wanted us to come here. No one else knows about the aliens. They probably want to capture us and put us in the prison on the moon. Then no one will be able to stop the invasion.'

'You're right,' said Kowalski. 'Let's go back in.'

Smith opened the door. 'He's gone!'

'He can't have got far!' said Kowalski. 'We need to find him.'

'Use the detector!' said Smith.

'The dot is moving very fast. They must have a car.'

'Let's get in our hired car and chase him.'

They ran to their car and got in. Kowalski started the car. Smith gave directions using the detector.

'This could be a trap, you know,' said Kowalski. 'We'd better be careful.'

Soon they arrived at the beach.

'There he is!' said Smith. They watched the journalist who was walking towards the sea. When he reached the water he didn't stop. He kept going.

'What's he doing?' said Smith.

'I don't know.'

Soon the journalist was completely underwater and they could no longer see him.

'How are we going to follow him?' wondered Kowalski.

'Let's get in that boat,' said Smith.

They ran down to the shore and got in the boat. Smith started the engine and they went in the direction of the journalist.

'What's that?' said Kowalski looking down into the water.

'A UFO!' said Smith. Under the water they could both see what seemed to be a UFO. It was a blue circular spacecraft with glowing green lines.

'Got any ideas?' asked Smith.

'If he gets into that UFO, he will take off and we won't be able to chase him any longer.'

While they were speaking, a strange whirring noise began from under the water.

'It's taking off!' said Smith. 'When I was saving you, I found a bottle containing a glowing liquid… perhaps some kind of weapon. We could throw it at the UFO's engine.'

'Good idea!' said Kowalski.

The boat started to shake in the water as the UFO began to lift off. As the UFO rose from the water, Smith threw the bottle at its engine. The bottle smashed against the side of the engine, and the purple liquid began to melt the metal coverings. The engine started making strange noises and sounded like it was overheating. The UFO started going down and crashed on the beach.

'Quick!' said Kowalski, 'He might try to escape.'

Smith drove the boat back to the shore and they both got out and examined the crash. They found the unconscious journalist lying in the UFO.

'Look, he is an alien!' said Smith. He pointed to the journalist's mask that was no longer on the alien's face. Instead of the mask, the alien had a green head with big bold black eyes.

'What do we do now?' asked Kowalski.

'We can't trust the cops, any of them could be aliens.' replied Smith.

'Let's take him back to our hotel room and question him.'

'OK, let's wait till it's dark so no-one will see us.'

Chapter Four: The Questioning

The hotel room had two single beds, a TV, two small glass tables, a cupboard in the corner, and a bathroom off to the side. In the middle was a circular table made out of glass, with two chairs. Sitting on one of the chairs was the alien who had been pretending to be a journalist. On the other chair was Kowalski. Smith was standing close by.

'What are you do to me?' asked the alien, trying to speak English.

'We are going to question you,' said Kowalski.

'What question about?'

'Why did you aliens imprison me on the moon?'

'Moon? Prison?'

'You know exactly what I'm talking about. You are going to stay here until you answer my questions. Did you imprison me because I'm a scientist?'

'You know lot of a science.'

'Were you trying to kidnap me again today?'

'No.'

'Where were you going to go in that UFO?'

'Going base to.'

'Going to what base?'

'Friendly base to. Aliens friendly are.'

'If you are friendly, then why did you kidnap me?'

The alien didn't reply but his skin started to dissolve.

'What's happening?' said Smith.

The alien turned into a pool of purple liquid. Only his clothes remained.

'We should search his clothes,' said Smith. In the pocket of the clothes they only found a receipt.

Kowalski read it. 'It's from a hotel in Florida. The alien base is probably in Florida.'

'Looks like we're going to Florida,' said Smith.

Two days later...

'I've never seen such a big hotel!' said Smith. Smith and Kowalski were about to go into the five star Miami Hotel, which they had learned about from the alien's receipt. The hotel had three swimming pools: two outdoors and one indoor. It had seven hundred rooms and five restaurants. They went into the reception.

'We'd like a room for two, please,' said Smith.

'Full we are,' said the receptionist.

'Are you sure there aren't any more rooms?' asked Kowalski.

'Have one we might,' said the receptionist, checking on the computer.

Smith and Kowalski looked at each other, puzzled.

'We have yes.'

'Yes, we'll take it,' said Kowalski.

'Number room 247,' said the receptionist handing them a key.

'Thank you,' said Smith.

Smith and Kowalski went into the elevator and the doors closed.

'That guy who gave us our room key sounded like an alien,' said Smith.

'Yes, he did,' replied Kowalski.

'Ding!' The elevator door opened, and Smith and Kowalski went to their room.

In the room, there was one chair and a glass coffee table facing the TV. There was one king size bed. Smith and Kowalski walked into the bathroom. In the bathroom there were two sinks, two baths and no toilet.

'Why are there two baths and no toilet?' asked Kowalski.

'And two sinks!' said Smith.

As they were speaking, there was a knock on the door.

'Should we answer it?' asked Kowalski. 'It could be a trap.'

'Cleaners hello!' came a voice from outside.

'I think we should let them in,' said Smith. 'They are just cleaners I think.'

Kowalski opened the door. Three women came in.

'Hello we clean,' said one of them.

One of the cleaners started cleaning the TV with a broom.

'Why is she cleaning the TV with a broom?' whispered Smith.

'I don't know,' said Kowalski.

Another cleaner used a feather duster on the bottom of the wooden chair. Ten minutes later they left.

'Maybe this place is run by aliens,' said Kowalski, 'because that is not what normal cleaners would do. I think we've come to the right place.'

Kowalski got out his detector and turned it on. After a few seconds, it showed two orange and four dozen green dots.

'This must be the alien base that the journalist alien was talking about,' said Smith.

'It must be,' said Kowalski.

‘Are there many other guests here?’ wondered Smith.

‘We didn’t see any when we checked in,’ said Kowalski. ‘And how would aliens afford to buy this five star hotel?’

‘I don’t know,’ said Smith. ‘We should go down at dinner time and explore to see if we are the only ones here and if this really is a hotel.’

At about six o’clock, they went down to one of the restaurants and found that it was full of people. They stood by a sign saying, ‘Seated wait here to be.’

‘That’s backwards!’ said Kowalski. ‘Maybe the people here are actually aliens. Maybe there are no real humans here besides us!’

‘That’s right, we only saw two orange pixels,’ said Smith. ‘Here we go. A waiter is coming over.’

'Your is ready table. Hello. Me follow.' said the waiter.

Smith and Kowalski followed the waiter to their table.

'Menus here are your,' said the waiter, and walked back into the kitchen.

'Isn't it a bit dangerous being around so many aliens?' whispered Kowalski.

'We need to find some proof that they are aliens. No one will believe your detector without proof.'

'You're right.'

The waiter returned. 'For you drinks?'

'Yes, please,' said Smith. 'I will have Purple Paradise.'

'And I will have lemonade,' said Kowalski.

'OK!' said the waiter and walked off.

'What's Purple Paradise?' asked Kowalski. 'I've never heard of that.'

'I don't know,' said Smith. 'It was the cheapest drink on the menu. Only 10¢.'

The waiter returned carrying a glass of purple liquid with steam coming out of it, and a glass of lemonade. He put the drinks on the table and left again.

'Isn't this meant to be a smoothie?' asked Smith. 'Why is there steam coming out of it?'

'I don't know, I thought the same as you. I'll try an experiment.'

Kowalski picked up Smith's spoon and dropped it in the purple liquid. Instantly, the spoon disintegrated.

'Acid!' said Kowalski. 'It must be the same liquid as in the baths on the moon.'

'I understand!' said Smith. 'These aliens in the hotel must think that we are aliens too. They can't tell us apart because their disguises make all aliens look like humans. That means we can explore the hotel in safety.'

'Maybe we need to start talking like aliens too,' said Kowalski.

'Idea good!' said Smith, smiling.

Chapter Five: Dungeons?

Kowalski finished his lemonade, and Smith took his drink to a bin and poured it in. The bottom of the bin disintegrated. They left the restaurant and started to explore.

'Let's go and look at the swimming pools,' said Kowalski.

When they got to the main pool, Smith noticed something. 'Why is that drain so big in the pool?'

'I don't think that is a drain,' said Kowalski.

'Then what is it?'

'Maybe we should look closer.'

They searched for some time but at first they didn't find anything suspicious.

'What's this sign?' asked Smith. He was pointing at a large red sign with white lettering. It read 'PULL LEVER IF EMERGENCY.' A chrome lever was attached to the side of the sign.

'Let's pull the lever,' said Smith. He pulled the lever and a loud creaking noise was heard from the bottom of the pool. They looked into the pool and saw the big drain opening. The water began to drain away.

'I've never seen a pool where the water drains away,' said Kowalski. Fifteen minutes later the pool had completely drained of water.

'Should we go in?' asked Kowalski.

'In the drain!' exclaimed Smith.

'I don't think it's a drain. I think it's a tunnel.'

They climbed down the ladder into the empty pool. Now they could see that there was a spiral staircase inside the drain.

'It might be a dungeon,' said Smith. 'They are aliens.'

'I have a torch in my back pocket,' said Kowalski.

'OK, let's go.'

Kowalski led the way as they slowly walked down the spiral staircase.

'It is a dungeon,' said Kowalski. 'Why would it say PULL LEVER IF EMERGENCY if it's a dungeon?'

'I don't know,' replied Smith.

The dungeon was a huge dark room with stone walls and a stone floor. There was no sound at all. Kowalski shone his torch on the walls, and saw some writing. Coloured in red and still wet was a number.

'What is that?' asked Smith.

'I don't know,' said Kowalski. 'It must have been very recent because the spray paint is still dripping. Someone must be here with us. And maybe trying to give us a clue.'

Smith wrote down the number in his notepad: 1144.

Suddenly they heard footsteps running up the spiral staircase. Kowalski shone his torch over in that direction but he was too late. Whoever it was had already gone.

'Quick! Up the staircase!' said Kowalski. They ran up the staircase and climbed back out into the pool.

'There he is!' said Smith, pointing at a figure dressed all in black who was running back into the main hotel building. They chased him into the building, but he had disappeared.

'Let's go to reception and ask if they saw that guy,' said Smith.

'Good idea,' replied Kowalski.

They jogged to the reception and Smith spoke to the receptionist, trying to use the alien way of speaking. 'Seen you have black in dressed a man?'

'Have I yes,' replied the receptionist.

'Way did he go which?' asked Kowalski.

'Into bar the,' said the receptionist.

Kowalski and Smith quickly ran to the bar.

'That's him, isn't it?' said Kowalski, pointing at a man with a black hoodie who was sitting at the bar. 'He's trying to fit in, hoping we don't notice him.'

As soon as the man realised he had been seen, he leapt off his stool and barged through Smith and Kowalski and ran out of the bar.

'Don't chase him! Look!' said Smith. He pointed to one of the booths along one wall of the bar. Each booth had a number over it. 'I think he brought us here on purpose. The booths are numbered 1… 2… 3… 4… 1144… 5 and so on.'

'Let's go and check out booth 1144,' said Kowalski.

They went over to the booth, sat down, and waited to see what would happen.

A man with a suit and tie came and sat opposite them. 'You I see want to join invasion the,' he said.

Smith and Kowalski looked confused.

'Invasion?' said Kowalski.

'Booth this is for joining the invasion Earth of,' said the man.

'Oh!' said Smith. 'We yes would like to join.'

'Keys for UFO here are.' The man handed Smith some keys. 'Remember no attack till ready all are.'

'OK,' said Kowalski.

'UFO the on roof is.'

'Thanks, OK,' said Smith.

Smith and Kowalski got up and went to the elevator in the hotel lobby. They looked at the buttons. The bottom button was marked D, then the buttons were numbered 1, 2, 3, 4, 5, 6, 7, 8, 9, and the top button was marked R.

'Hold on,' said Kowalski. 'Isn't it supposed to say B at the bottom, for basement?'

'D is probably for dungeon!' said Smith.

'Yes, probably.'

Smith pressed the button named R – for Roof – and the elevator started moving.

'DING!' The elevator doors opened and Smith and Kowalski walked out on to the roof.

Chapter Six: The Test Flight

On the roof there were four pads, and three of them had a UFO parked on them.

'Let's give it a test drive,' said Kowalski.

'Good idea,' said Smith. 'How do we get in?'

Kowalski pressed a button on the keys and the glass dome at the top of one of the UFOs opened.

'Cool!' said Smith.

Smith and Kowalski got in the UFO. There were four chairs in the cockpit and one of the chairs had the controls in front of it. Smith sat in the pilot's seat and Kowalski sat behind him.

'How do you know how to fly this again?' asked Kowalski.

'I've flown dozens of planes and helicopters, I'll easily figure it out,' replied Smith.

Kowalski used the keys to close the glass dome and Smith started the engine. He lifted off the roof and started to fly upwards.

'Let's fly to Miami Beach!' said Kowalski.

'OK,' said Smith, 'I should turn the invisibility on.'

'Invisibility?' asked Kowalski.

'So no one will see us.' Smith pulled a lever labelled 'Invisibility Drive.'

The UFO vanished, and Smith flew towards Miami Beach. Two minutes later, Smith set the UFO to hover over the beach.

'Here we are!' said Smith. 'Let's check out the weapons.'

'Weapons?' said Kowalski.

'Do you not know UFOs have weapons? They wouldn't be able to invade if they didn't have weapons on their UFOs. We need to know what weapons they have so we can stop them.'

Smith looked at the controls. 'I think these are rockets. We can't use them on the beach because there are people.'

'Let's fire one into the sea,' said Kowalski.

There were four numbered buttons on the control panel. Smith pressed number four. The rocket made a loud noise as it was fired. When it hit the sea, a huge area of water instantly disappeared. Water all around it filled in the empty hole. On the nearby beach, people started screaming and running, not knowing what was happening.

'This is much more powerful than any rocket on Earth,' said Smith. He sounded alarmed.

'We need to alert the authorities,' said Kowalski.

'But they won't believe us,' said Smith.

'We have this UFO as proof now,' replied Kowalski.

'We should go and see the President.'

'Won't we get shot down if we fly to the White House?'

'Not if we have the invisibility drive on,' said Smith. 'Let's fly to Washington DC. The journey will take about five hours.'

Kowalski sighed. He didn't like long journeys.

Five hours later…

It was 9.32pm when Smith gently landed the invisible UFO on the White House lawn.

'How are we going to get in to see the President?' asked Smith. 'He doesn't even know we're coming.'

'I think we should try and sneak in,' replied Kowalski.

'But there's so much security. What if we get caught?'

'We won't!' said Kowalski. During the flight, Kowalski had investigated the UFO and had found a flap. Behind the flap was a ray gun which could fire a freeze ray. Kowalski leaned out of the UFO and aimed the ray gun at the fountain in the middle of the White House lawn. He fired and the fountain instantly froze. All the guards quickly ran to the fountain to investigate.

'Quick!' said Kowalski, 'Now's our chance.'

Smith and Kowalski quickly ran to the front door of the White House.

'How are we going to get in?' asked Smith.

Kowalski fired the ray gun at the White House door and then kicked it and the door fell down. They ran in.

'Are there guards in here as well?' asked Smith.

'There are.' Kowalski got out his detector.

'Why are you looking for aliens?' asked Smith.

'Who knows? The President might be an alien.' The display showed only orange dots. 'Everyone here is human.'

'Good,' said Smith.

'And look,' said Kowalski. 'There are three orange dots in one place. I think that must be the President and his guards.'

'It probably is,' said Smith. 'Let's walk towards the orange dots.'

'OK.' said Kowalski.

Smith and Kowalski followed the orange dots.

'I think this is the dining room,' said Smith as they came close to the orange dots on the detector. 'How are we going to get in? The two guards will be near the door.'

‘Time for another distraction,’ whispered Kowalski. He fired the freeze ray at another door, and it fell down with a crash. Two guards ran out of the dining room to investigate the noise.

‘Quick, we've got to go now,’ said Smith.

They ran into the dining room. The President looked up alarmed. He was sitting at a large dining table.

‘Mr President,’ said Smith, ‘I am Captain Ali Smith and this is Professor Sam Kowalski. We have urgent information about the fate of the whole planet.’

‘The fate of the whole planet?’ asked the President.

‘Aliens are going to invade,’ explained Smith.

‘Do you have any proof?’

'Yes. We have parked an invisible UFO on your front lawn.'

'A UFO!' exclaimed the President.

'We also have this,' said Kowalski, handing over the ray gun.

'What does it do?'

'It freezes things. And I have also built a detector to detect aliens. They can disguise themselves perfectly as humans.'

While they were speaking, the guards rushed back in. 'Hands up!' they said, aiming their guns at Smith and Kowalski.

'Stop!' ordered the President. 'Bring these men onto the front lawn.'

'OK, sir,' said one of the guards.

A minute later, they were on the front lawn.

'Where's the UFO?' asked the President.

'It's still in invisible drive,' said Kowalski.

'What's invisible drive?' asked the President.

'It turns the UFO invisible,' said Kowalski. 'It's one of the many alien inventions they are planning to use to invade the Earth.' Kowalski took the UFO keys out of his pocket and turned off the invisibility drive. The UFO appeared.

The President and the guards gasped.

'You were telling the truth!' said the President. 'How long have we got until they invade?'

'We don't know,' said Smith.

'We might not have much time till they invade,' said Kowalski. 'So we need to start working on the Earth's defences.'

'How many aliens are there?' asked the President.

'We've seen a few hundred,' said Smith. 'That doesn't mean there aren't more of them.'

'I'm going to call a meeting at the Pentagon,' said the President. 'I want you guys to come along as you're alien experts.'

'I don't know about that,' said Smith. 'But we'll help in any way we can.'

'If we can't stop them, who knows what will happen,' said Kowalski.

Smith and Kowalski got into their UFO and waved at the President. 'See you at the Pentagon!' said Smith. He took off and the UFO disappeared into the night sky behind the White House.

Chapter Seven: The Meeting

The large meeting room had screens along one wall. Sitting around a big table were the President, five generals, Smith, and Kowalski.

'How you do know the aliens want to invade?' asked the President.

'I found out about it on the moon,' said Kowalski.

'I think aliens friendly are,' said the President. 'I don't think they invade will.'

Smith and Kowalski looked at each other with amazed expressions. Why was the President saying this?

At that moment, another President walked into the room with two security guards.

'Arrest that alien!' said both Presidents simultaneously.

'Alien?' asked Smith.

'I'm the real President,' said the President who had just entered the room.

'No, I'm the President real,' insisted the President sitting at the table.

'I'll use my detector,' said Kowalski. A few moments later, he found the answer. 'This is an alien sitting at the table!'

The two security guards dragged the alien away. 'I back will be!' shouted the alien.

'We need to be careful,' said Kowalski. 'Anyone we see could be an alien.'

'We need to start making more bombs,' said the senior general, General Jones.

'There's no point in making bombs,' said Kowalski. 'When they go invisible we won't be able to see them and our bombs will be useless.'

'So what can we do?' asked the President.

'Order pizza?' asked Smith. 'We might think better if we aren't hungry.'

'This is too urgent,' said the President. 'Let's make a plan first.'

Smith sighed. 'Can we hack in?'

'Good idea!' said Kowalski. 'Bring us a laptop.'

'And some pizza!' added Smith.

Seventy minutes later…

'It's no good,' said Kowalski, finishing his slice of pizza. 'We can't hack in from here. There's too much security on the alien systems.'

'Is there anything we can do?' asked the President.

'We need to turn off the alien security systems. They must be in a base somewhere on Earth connected to our networks.'

'How can we find this alien base?' asked General Jones.

'Can you use your satellite cameras?' asked Smith.

'Great idea,' said the President. 'General, find the alien base. Get all the military working on it. Use every satellite we've got.'

Two days later…

'We've found the alien base!' said General Jones.

'Where is it?' asked Kowalski.

'In the desert, where I do not know.'

'So have we got to search the entire desert?'

'I'm afraid so.'

'We'd better get going,' said Smith.

'Let's get in the UFO,' said Kowalski.

'UFO?' said General Jones.

'Yes, UFO. We found it on the roof of a hotel in Florida.' said Kowalski. 'We can use it to locate the base in the desert. We will be able to find it quite quickly because we will be very high up.'

Smith, Kowalski, General Jones, and the President got in the UFO and flew off.

Chapter Eight: The Alien Base

‘We’ve been searching for so long and found nothing,’ said Smith.

‘It’s just sand,’ said General Jones.

‘Are you sure it’s here?’ asked Smith.

‘Yes, I’m sure,’ said General Jones.

One hour later…

'Slow down, what's this grey building?' said the President.

'Maybe it's the alien base?' said Kowalski. 'I will turn the invisibility drive on.'

'Invisibility drive? It goes invisible?' asked General Jones.

'Yes!' said Kowalski.

They landed the invisible UFO next to the grey building. They got out and right in from of them was a big steel armoured door.

'How are we supposed to get inside?' asked the President.

'Look,' said Kowalski. 'There's a control panel.'

'We need a code,' said General Jones.

'Maybe knock?' said Smith.

'Knock, are you mad?' said Kowalski. 'We're trying to sneak in and not get caught.'

'I could pretend to be the alien President,' said the President.

'You would have to put words in the wrong order. That is how they speak,' said Kowalski.

'This like?' said the President.

'Yes, perfect!' said Kowalski. 'We'll go and hide in the invisible UFO. You go invisible when you get in.'

'Very cool,' said General Jones.

When they were in position, the President knocked. 'I hope this works,' he muttered to himself.

A security guard opened the door. 'Welcome, President. Have got you information the?'

'Yes. I need to the boss report to.'

'Come in.'

The President entered the alien base. Inside there were lots of people walking around in different directions. Kowalski, Smith, and General Jones sneaked out of the UFO and got into the alien base before the door closed. They quickly hid behind a cabinet.

'Why are there so many people?' said Kowalski, alarmed. 'Where has the President gone?'

'I think he went down there,' said Smith.

'Down those stairs?'

'Yes,' said Smith.

'There is a pencil on top of the cabinet,' said Kowalski. 'I will throw that at one of the aliens to distract them.'

The pencil hit the alien's head.

'Did that who?!' the alien shouted.

'Me not!' the other aliens shouted back.

The aliens started arguing.

'Now's our time,' said Kowalski. 'Run across down the stairs, but be careful, there might be more down there.'

'I hope the President's OK,' said Smith.

They ran to the other side of the room and down the stairs. There was nobody there.

'He's not down here,' said Kowalski.

'Maybe they've figured out that he's not an alien,' said General Jones. 'There are some more stairs. Why don't we go down them?'

‘Maybe that’s where the President is,’ said Kowalski.

They walked halfway down the stairs and stopped. There was a small room packed full of green tubes each big enough to hold a human, and they saw that the President was inside one!

‘It’s the President! Is he all right?’ said Smith.

‘Look, there are other people in them as well!’ said General Jones. ‘But no one else here.’

‘Let’s go see if he’s okay,’ said Smith. They walked down the stairs into the small room and walked up to the President. Inside the tube, the President was motionless.

‘He looks like he’s asleep,’ said Kowalski.

‘How do we get him out of this tube?’ said Smith.

'Why don't we rescue everybody?' said Kowalski.

'How do we know they are all humans?' said General Jones.

'We know the President is a human, so therefore everyone else is probably a human as well,' said Kowalski. 'If we set everyone free to escape, in the chaos, we can find a way to disable the security system.'

'Yes, but if they are asleep, how are we supposed to wake them up?' said General Jones.

'What's this?' said Smith, pointing to a red button on the wall.

'What do you think?' said Kowalski. 'It's a red button. If you push it, it will probably set off an alarm.'

'It's weird that it's just out in the open, anyone could push it,' said General Jones.

'I have a plan,' said Kowalski. 'General Jones, you wait here and in ten minutes press the red button, then help the President and all the prisoners to escape. Meanwhile, Smith and I will find the security system and disable it.'

Smith and Kowalski sneaked down a dark, dingy, dirty tunnel with eery noises.

'This doesn't look like it's the way to the computer room.' said Smith.

'The computer room must be hidden away so it's protected,' said Kowalski. 'It's where all their information is. It wouldn't be right by the front door.'

'Good point.' said Smith.

They walked a long way. The ten minutes was nearly up when they came to a door in the side of the tunnel. It was a thick metal door like the door to a bank vault.

'How do we get in?' asked Smith.

Kowalski tried opening the door but it didn't budge. Then suddenly the alarm went off.

'Quick, hide!' said Kowalski.

'There is nowhere to hide!' said Smith.

'Let's hide behind the door as it opens,' said Kowalski.

The door opened and six aliens ran out. They didn't see Kowalski and Smith as they ran past in a panic. When they were out of sight, Kowalski and Smith cautiously went into the room.

Inside was a very big room with lots of different computers. There were no aliens left in the room.

'How are we supposed to figure out how to disable the security system?' shouted Smith over the piercingly loud sound of the alarm.

Kowalski took a memory stick out of his pocket and inserted it into the nearest computer.

'It's a virus!' he shouted. 'It will disable their security system! They won't be smart enough to delete one of my viruses!'

Smith and Kowalski ran out of the room and back towards the entrance of the base. On the way they passed aliens who were still panicking, but no one paid any attention to them. When they got to the main door of the base, it was open. Aliens were running outside in the panic, worried that the base was on fire. Kowalski saw General Jones and the President. In the panic, none of the aliens had noticed that the President had escaped.

All four of them ran out of the door, and climbed into the invisible UFO.

'We disabled the security system,' said Kowalski, as they climbed into their seats.

'I set off the alarm just as we planned,' explained General Jones. 'I didn't know where you were, but it seems to have worked OK. I set free everyone in the tubes. They knew where the aliens had taken their cars which they had been driving when they were captured, so they were able to escape that way. The President and I ran back to the main door which is when we saw you. With all the aliens running in a panic we blended in and ran out with them.'

'Now I've put a virus into the alien security system, we should be able to hack into it.' said Kowalski.

'Let's go back to the Pentagon,' said the President. 'We can hack in from there.'

Chapter Nine: Showdown

'I've done it! I've hacked in!' exclaimed Kowalski.

Smith, the President, and General Jones ran over to Kowalski's monitor.

'That's great,' said the President.

'What should I do now?' asked Kowalski. 'I now have the codes to all the doors in every alien base, and I have lots of information about UFOs and about the aliens' plans for invading.'

'Now we know their weaknesses we should attack,' said General Jones.

'Or we could meet up with the alien boss,' said Smith, 'and tell him not to invade. We can tell him there's no chance of success now we know all the information from hacking in.'

'I think we should try Smith's idea,' decided the President. 'And if that doesn't work, then we can attack.'

'I can probably identify which UFO belongs to the alien boss,' said Kowalski. 'If I can take control of it, I can make it land here at the Pentagon.'

'I think that's a good plan,' said the President. 'We've just got to hope the alien boss will be in the UFO. General Jones, make sure the UFO doesn't get shot down when it lands.'

'Yes, sir!' replied General Jones. 'And I'll make sure there are plenty of guards standing by.'

'It's a lot of work for Kowalski,' said Smith. 'Can we get some more pizza?'

One hour later…

Outside, at the Pentagon landing pad, Smith, Kowalski, General Jones, and the President were standing waiting, and five guards were standing nearby. Kowalski was holding a controller.

'The alien boss should be landing in the UFO soon,' said Kowalski, as he operated the controller.

'Is that dot the UFO?' asked Smith, pointing to a black dot in the azure blue sky.

'I think that's it,' said Kowalski.

'So what do we do when it lands?' asked General Jones.

'We can use the freeze ray,' said Kowalski.

'While the alien boss is frozen I will question him,' said the President. 'And tell him we know all his plans and how to defeat him.'

As the UFO flew nearer, they could see it more clearly. It looked just like the UFO which Smith and Kowalski had been flying in. Using the controller, Kowalski made the UFO land just in front of them.

Four green-skinned aliens climbed out of the UFO. For once they weren't wearing human disguises. The first one was obviously the alien leader. He was much bigger than the others and was wearing a royal purple cloak. Next to him was an alien wearing a black hoodie with the hood up. Behind them were two alien guards.

'Who are you?' shouted the alien leader. 'Who is controlling my UFO?' It seemed the boss aliens could speak English normally.

Before hearing another sentence, Kowalski fired the freeze ray four times in quick succession. All four aliens were frozen.

'Well done, Kowalski,' said the President. Turning to the aliens, he said, 'You will be frozen for around fifteen minutes and you are going to listen me. You probably know who I am. I am the President of the United States of America. We've disabled your security system and hacked in to your computers. We know all your secrets. We know how your weapons and UFOs work and know your plans to invade. There's no way that you can succeed now. You must surrender and make peace with us. I will give you a few minutes, while the ice melts, to think over your decision.'

A few minutes later, the ice had melted enough so that the alien leader was able to talk again. He was even angrier than before.

'I don't care that you know my secrets. I will just send even more UFOs to invade. You might know how they work, but there's nothing you can do if you are outnumbered!'

'Wait a minute!' said Smith. 'I'm pretty sure I recognize that black hoodie with red paint on the sleeve. He's the one who helped us get our UFO, back in the hotel.'

'What!' cried the alien leader, turning to the alien dressed in black. 'You helped them get the UFO? They know how our UFOs and weapons work because of you?'

The alien in black stepped forward. 'That's right,' he said. 'I've been helping the humans behind the scenes.' He turned to Kowalski and Smith. 'The chances of you landing at the exact area where Moonbase is were very low. So I hacked into your systems and made sure you would land within twenty-five metres of the base. Later I made sure you would get your own UFO– that's when I got the spray paint on my sleeve.'

'You're supposed to be my assistant!' shouted the alien leader. 'Why don't you want us to invade?'

'We don't need to invade. All this killing is unnecessary. We have our own planet. We should live peacefully with the humans.'

The alien leader looked even angrier than ever. 'I will send you to the prison in Moonbase for the rest of your life.'

'No you won't!' said General Jones. 'Guards! Take him away!' The guards handcuffed the alien leader and the two alien guards. They were taken away into the Pentagon.

'What now?' asked Smith.

'I have an idea,' said the President. 'This alien in black should be the new leader of the aliens. He wants peace between humans and aliens, and so do we.'

'I agree,' said Kowalski.

'So do I,' said Smith.

'That would be great,' said the alien in black. 'I can teach all the aliens how to live peacefully with humans. Some of them can stay on the Earth, but as friends not enemies.'

'That is a good idea,' said Kowalski. 'We'll make sure that the newspapers and TV stations tell everyone that the aliens are friendly. General Jones and I will help the aliens to settle in to their new life on Earth.'

'I will take you to our base straight away,' said the alien in black. 'We can get started.'

The alien in black, Kowalski, and General Jones got into the UFO and flew off.

Smith turned to the President. 'Looks like there's no invasion any time soon.'

'In that case,' said the President, 'would you like a promotion? I need a new pilot for Air Force One.'

'You're offering me the job?' asked Smith. 'I'd be honoured.'

The President and Smith shook hands, and walked back into the Pentagon together.

Printed in Great Britain
by Amazon

35802725R00057